Fantastic Folk Tales

THE PRINCE AND THE DOVE

Spanish Folk Tale

An imprint of Om Books International

Once upon a time, there was a prosperous little Kingdom in ancient Mexico, governed by a just King. The King had one son. When the prince was of a marriageable age, the King started to look for a suitable bride for him.

However, the prince told his parents, "I want to marry the most beautiful woman in the whole world. Therefore, I am going to journey all over the world until I find her."

The king agreed to the prince's proposal and the prince left for his journey across the world.

During his journey, he came to a fountain where he stopped to take a drink. As the prince bent over to drink, he saw a reflection of three oranges in the water. Looking up, he saw three large and beautiful oranges on the branch of a tree.

How tasty they look, thought the prince. Climbing the tree, he plucked the oranges from the branch. He sat down under the tree. As he cut the first orange in half, a beautiful maiden appeared from the fruit.

"Give me bread," said the maiden to the prince. "I can't," he answered, "because I don't have any."

The maiden became very sad. "Then to my orange I will return," said the maiden. Saying so, she vanished and the orange became whole again.

The prince cut the second orange, and from this fruit also sprang a maiden, much more beautiful than the first. "Give me bread," the second maiden told the prince.
"I can't," said he, "because I don't have any."

"Then to my orange I will return," said the maiden, and the orange became whole again. The prince thoughtfully considered the situation. He decided to get some bread before he cut the third orange lest another maiden appeared asking for it.

As the prince was wondering what to do, a gypsy passed by in a cart. "Wait!" cried the prince and ran after the cart. He approached the gypsy and said, "I will give you a golden coin for a piece of bread." The gypsy willingly gave him some bread.

The prince happily cut the third orange. And from the orange sprang a maiden, much more beautiful than the other two. "Give me bread," the third maiden said. The prince joyously gave her bread. The maiden of the orange then exclaimed, "Thank you for the bread. What can I do for you?"

"Marry me," answered the prince. He noticed that the maiden was wearing shabby clothes and told her, "Remain here with this gypsy, while I go and bring some good clothes for you."

The gypsy's daughter saw the prince riding away and fell in love with him. She told her father that she wanted to marry the prince. The gypsy girl approached the maiden and said, "Let me comb your hair so that you will look much more beautiful when the prince returns."

The maiden graciously agreed. As the gypsy girl began combing, she stuck a pin in the maiden's head. Immediately, the maiden turned into a dove and the gypsy girl took her place with the help of her father.

Soon, the prince returned and, seeing the gypsy girl, exclaimed, "How dark you have become!" "The sun has burnt my skin," she answered. The prince, believing the gypsy girl to be the maiden, took her to his palace.

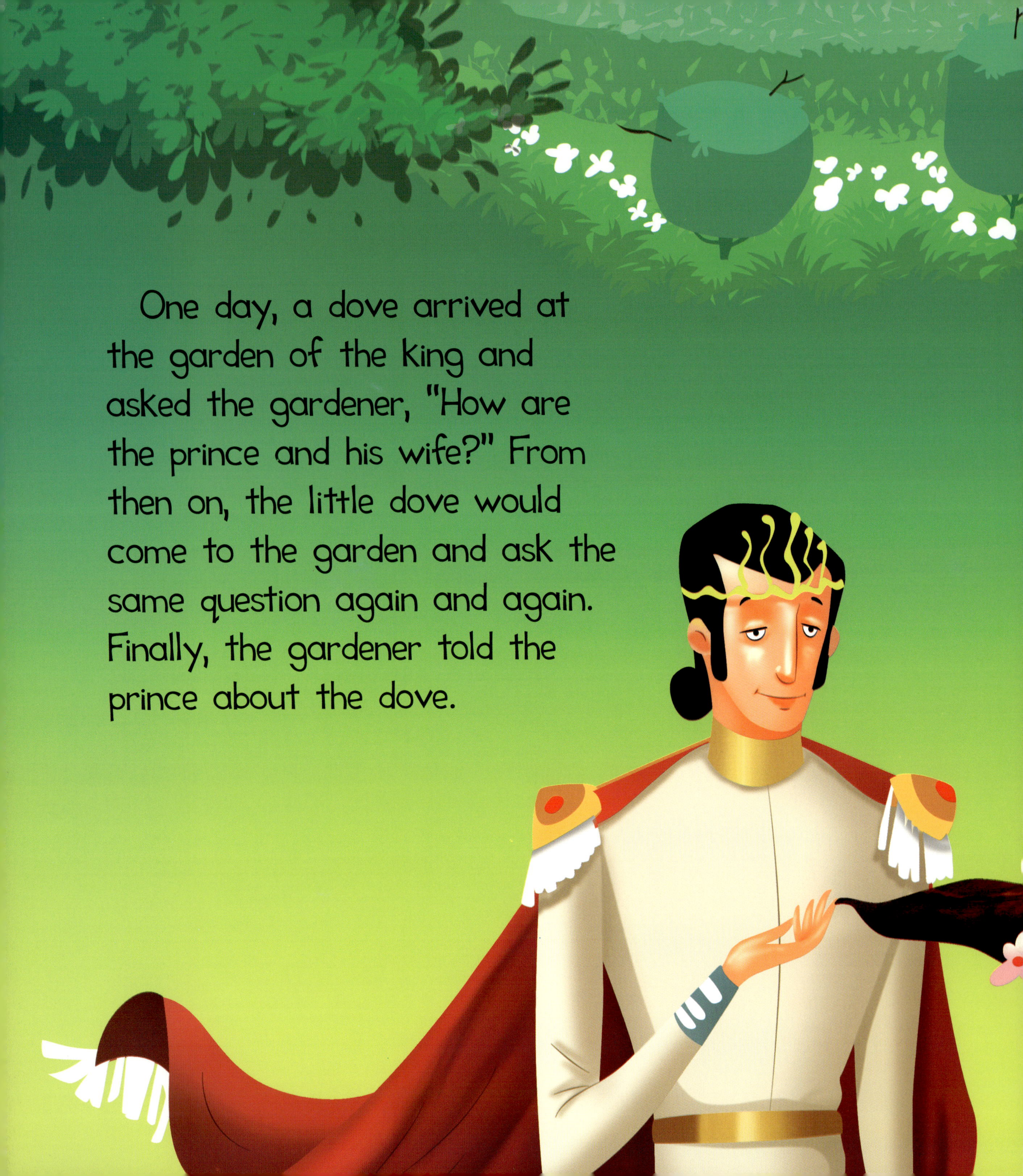

One day, a dove arrived at the garden of the king and asked the gardener, "How are the prince and his wife?" From then on, the little dove would come to the garden and ask the same question again and again. Finally, the gardener told the prince about the dove.

The prince then ordered him to capture the bird next time it came to the garden. The prince fell in love with the little dove as soon as he saw it. He took the bird in his hands and began stroking its head. Feeling the pin in the dove's head, he jerked it out. Immediately, the dove changed back into the maiden of the orange.

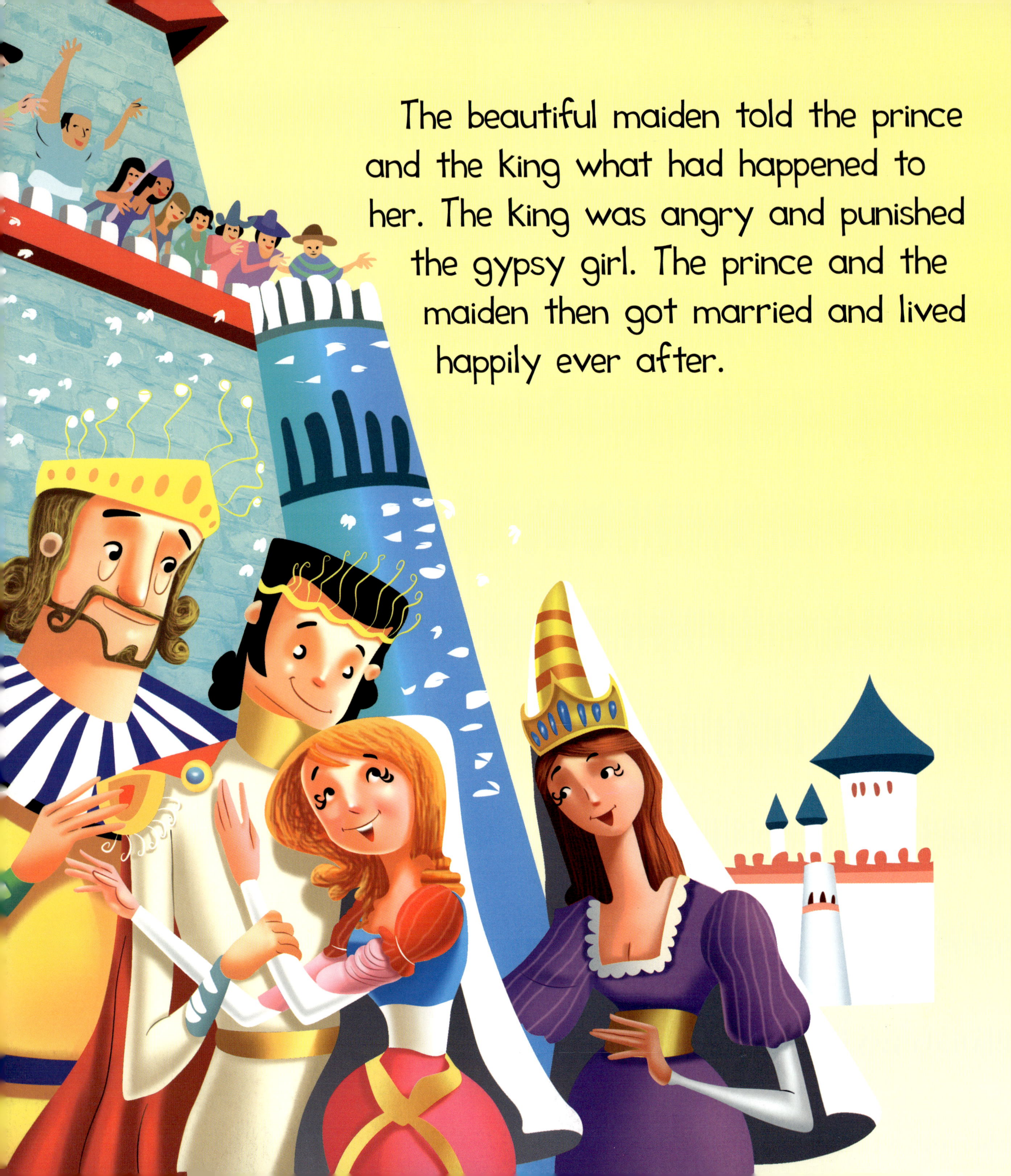

The beautiful maiden told the prince and the King what had happened to her. The King was angry and punished the gypsy girl. The prince and the maiden then got married and lived happily ever after.